Duck is Stuck

and

Get the Ball!

Maverick
Early Readers

'Duck is Stuck' and 'Get the Ball!'
An original concept by Katie Dale
© Katie Dale

Illustrated by Serena Lombardo

Published by MAVERICK ARTS PUBLISHING LTD
Studio 11, City Business Centre, 6 Brighton Road,
Horsham, West Sussex, RH13 5BB
© Maverick Arts Publishing Limited August 2019
+44 (0)1403 256941

A CIP catalogue record for this book is available at the British Library.

ISBN 978-1-84886-613-3

www.maverickbooks.co.uk

This book is rated as: Pink Band (Guided Reading)
This story is decodable at Letters and Sounds Phase 2.

Duck is Stuck

and

Get the Ball!

By Katie Dale

Illustrated by
Serena Lombardo

The Letter S

Trace the lower and upper case letter with a finger. Sound out the letter.

Around, around

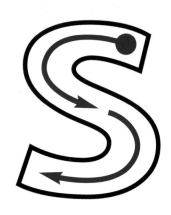

Around, around

Some words to familiarise:

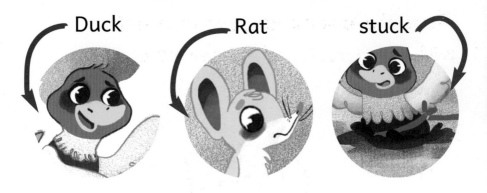

Duck   Rat   stuck

High-frequency words:

is not

Tips for Reading 'Duck is Stuck'

- Practise the words listed above before reading the story.

- If the reader struggles with any of the other words, ask them to look for sounds they know in the word. Encourage them to sound out the words and help them read the words if necessary.

- After reading the story, ask the reader who is stuck at the end of the story.

Fun Activity

Discuss how the animals were able to get Duck unstuck.

Duck is Stuck

Duck is stuck.

Tug, Rat, tug!

Duck is still stuck.

Tug, Cat, tug!

Duck is still stuck.

Tug, Dog, tug!

Duck is still stuck.

Tug, Rabbit, tug!

Duck is not stuck!

But Rat is stuck!

The Letter G

Trace the lower and upper case letter with a finger. Sound out the letter.

Around,
up,
down,
around

Around,
up,
lift,
cross

Some words to familiarise:

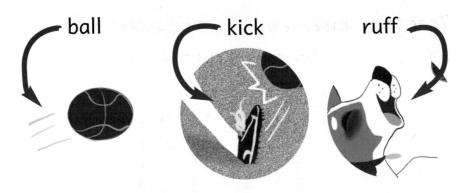

ball   kick   ruff

High-frequency words:

the

Tips for Reading 'Get the Ball!'

- Practise the words listed above before reading the story.

- If the reader struggles with any of the other words, ask them to look for sounds they know in the word. Encourage them to sound out the words and help them read the words if necessary.

- After reading the story, ask the reader which games the dog went through to get the ball.

Fun Activity

What was your favourite game in the story?

Get the Ball!

Toss the ball!

Hit the ball!

Tap the ball!

Kick the ball!

Get the ball!

Toss the ball!

Book Bands for Guided Reading

The Institute of Education book banding system is a scale of colours that reflects the various levels of reading difficulty. The bands are assigned by taking into account the content, the language style, the layout and phonics. Word, phrase and sentence level work is also taken into consideration.

Maverick Early Readers are a bright, attractive range of books covering the pink to white bands. All of these books have been book banded for guided reading to the industry standard and edited by a leading educational consultant.

Pink

Red

Yellow

Blue

Green

Orange

Turquoise

Purple

Gold

White

To view the whole Maverick Readers scheme, visit our website at
www.maverickearlyreaders.com

Or scan the QR code above to view our scheme instantly!